# I AM SHE-RA!

By **JOHN SAZAKLIS**

Illustrated by **SHANE CLESTER**

A GOLDEN BOOK • NEW YORK

SHE-RA and the Princesses of Power © 2019 DreamWorks Animation LLC. SHE-RA and associated trademarks and character copyrights are owned by and used under license from Mattel, Inc. Under license to Classic Media. All rights reserved. Published by Golden Books, an imprint of Random House Children's Books, a division of Penguin Random House LLC, 1745 Broadway, New York, NY 10019, and in Canada by Penguin Random House Canada Limited, Toronto. Golden Books, A Golden Book, A Little Golden Book, the G colophon, and the distinctive gold spine are registered trademarks of Penguin Random House LLC.
rhcbooks.com
ISBN 978-1-9848-5035-5 (trade) — ISBN 978-1-9848-5036-2 (ebook)
Printed in the United States of America
10 9 8 7 6 5 4 3 2 1

**W**elcome to Etheria!
I am **ADORA**, and this is my horse, **SPIRIT**.

I am a skilled warrior. I used to lead an evil army known as the **Horde**. The Horde serves the horrible **Hordak**.

One day, a warrior showed me the magical **Sword of Protection**. He said it belonged to me and had great power.

I thought he was a spy. I had him locked up at the Horde base known as the **Fright Zone**.

Suddenly, the **Sorceress of Castle Grayskull** appeared. "Adora," she said, "you are meant to become **SHE-RA, PRINCESS OF POWER**. The Horde placed you under a spell to serve evil instead of good. The Sword of Protection is your key to freedom!"

I held my sword high and said . . .

My sword also turned Spirit into the flying unicorn **SWIFT WIND**.

I told Swift Wind we had to rescue the stranger who had given me the sword.

The Sorceress said his name was **HE-MAN**— and he was my twin brother!

I used my super-strength to free him.

Suddenly, Hordak and the evil witch
**Shadow Weaver** attacked.
They were no match for me and
my brother!

Deep in the **Whispering Woods**, we found a band of
warriors called the **Great Rebellion**. They fight to free Etheria
from the evil forces of Hordak. Their leader, **Princess Glimmer**,
was with the amazing archer **Bow**, his flying friend **Kowl**,
and the magical **Madame Razz** and **Broom**.

Glimmer planned to take back **Castle Bright Moon** from the Horde and return the throne to her mother, **Queen Angella**. He-Man and I promised to help them.

Along with the Great Rebellion,
we charged into battle.
"For Castle Bright Moon!"
yelled Glimmer.

The new Horde leader, **Catra**, met us with her army.

Queen Angella was trapped in the tallest tower by a guard named **Hunga**. He-Man and I climbed inside. My brother freed the queen while I handled the horrible harpy.

We make a great team!

# WE HAVE THE POWER!

Queen Angella flew across the battlefield
blasting beams of magical light energy.
Defeated, Catra and her army returned
to the Fright Zone.

Castle Bright Moon was a happy place again!

Queen Angella sat on her throne with Princess Glimmer by her side.

The rebels celebrated with a fantastic feast!

Madame Razz cooked up a magical meal. Bow played a
beautiful song, and **Frosta** created an incredible ice sculpture.

Soon it was time for He-Man to go back to
Castle Grayskull. I told my brother I would visit
him once my work on Etheria was finished.

Now *I* am the leader of the Great Rebellion.
**I AM THE PRINCESS OF POWER**.